The Little Matchgirl

It was New Year's Eve in the old city and it was almost night. A poor girl walked the cold, dark streets in her bare feet. In the morning, she had been wearing a pair of her mother's slippers, but they were too big for her. She had lost them as she crossed a road, hurrying to get out of the way of two carts. The girl's parents had filled the pockets of her apron with matches and sent her out to sell them. All day, the little girl had trudged through the city, but no one had bought any.

It began to snow, but the girl was too tired to brush the flakes from her hair. All she could think of was how cold and hungry she felt.

She rested in a doorway, trying to keep out of the wind.

"If I go home before I've sold any matches, Father will be angry and he'll beat me," she thought.

She looked at her throbbing fingers. The cold had made them blue.

"I'll strike one match," thought the girl. "Only one, to warm my hands."

She took a match and struck it on the wall beside her. As the match spluttered and burned, its flame seemed to turn into a log fire, blazing in a polished brass hearth. The little girl smiled, stretched out her hands to the fire – and the match went out. The burning logs and gleaming hearth vanished in a flurry of snowflakes.

"Just one more," the girl whispered.

When she struck the second match, its flame seemed to shine right through the wall. The little girl could see into a room where a table was laid for dinner.

There were china plates and crystal glasses, and in the middle of the table a roast goose sizzled in a pan – and then the match went out. There was nothing to see but the cold brick wall.

The girl lit another match. This
time, she seemed to be sitting under
a Christmas tree. Parcels hung from its
branches and the whole tree was
decorated with tiny
lights. The little
girl reached out
her hands –
and the match
went out.

The tree
disappeared
and the lights
became the
stars, twinkling
in the sky.

One of the
stars fell, flashing
as it went.

"Grandmother
told me to make
a wish whenever
I saw a falling
star," said the
little girl; but
she was too
cold to think
of wishes.

She struck another match and saw its flame shine in the eyes of her grandmother, who stood before her.

"I thought you were dead, Grandmother!" cried the little girl. "Please don't leave me when the match goes out! Stay with me!"

Quickly, she lit the rest of the matches. They seemed to burn brighter than sunshine. As they flared up, the little girl saw her grandmother smile and felt her grandmother's arms around her, keeping her warm and safe.

In the morning, someone found the little matchgirl, still sitting on the doorstep with burnt matches scattered all around her. She had frozen to death in the night, but on her face was a smile as radiant as the sun that was rising above the rooftops.

The
Wild Swans

In the land where the swallows go in winter, there lived a king who had eleven sons and one daughter, Elisa. The princes and the princess knew nothing but happiness until the day the king married again.

The new queen was beautiful, but evil. She sent Elisa away to live with poor farmers in the country and she told so many awful lies about the young princes, that the king came to hate them.

The queen cast a spell over the princes.

"Wander through the world as songless birds!" she screeched.

The princes turned into eleven wild swans. They flew out of the castle and over the great green forest that stretched as far as the sea.

Elisa knew nothing about what had happened to her brothers. She lived and worked on the farm until she was fifteen, when her father asked to see her.

She was met at the palace gates by the queen. When the queen saw how beautiful Elisa was, she grew deadly jealous.

"You must have a bath before you meet your father, my dear," she told Elisa, with a false smile.

In the royal bathroom, the queen took three toads from inside her cloak. She kissed each one and said, "Sit on Elisa's eyes and make her ugly; sit on her head and make her stupid; sit on her heart and make her evil."

The queen dropped the toads into the bathwater, which went a strange green colour.

Elisa took her bath. The toads sat
on her eyes and head and heart, but
the young princess was so good that
evil magic could not harm her. The
toads turned into red poppies and
floated on the water.

The queen was furious when she
saw this. She streaked
Elisa's face with
walnut juice.

"This will make
you even more
beautiful for your
father," she told the girl.

Then she rubbed
ashes through Elisa's hair.

"This will make
your hair shine,"
the queen smiled.

The king was shocked when he saw
how dirty and ugly Elisa looked.

"Send her away," he said. "I never
want to see her again."

Elisa left the palace, weeping bitter
tears. She wished her brothers were
with her to comfort her, but they had
disappeared.

"Father must have sent them away,
too," she thought. "I'm going to search
until I find them."

And so Elisa wandered into the great green forest. For two days and two nights, Elisa travelled through the forest without seeing anyone. Then, on the morning of the third day, she met an old woman gathering berries.

"Have you seen eleven princes riding through the forest?" Elisa asked.

"No," replied the old woman, "but I've seen eleven swans with gold crowns on their heads, swimming in that stream over there. Follow the stream down to the sea and you may find what you are searching for."

Elisa followed the stream, hoping to see the mysterious swans; but she saw nothing, and at last the stream flowed out into the ocean, and Elisa could walk no further. She sat on the shore and cried with disappointment, but after a while she dried her tears.

"When the waves stop rolling, I'll give up looking for my brothers, but not until then!" she said to herself.

She watched the waves. On the far horizon, the sun was beginning to dip into the sea. As the sky turned red with sunset, Elisa saw eleven white swans, crowned with gold, flying towards her.

They landed beside her, and as the
last of the sun slipped out of sight, the
swans turned into Elisa's brothers. They
hugged her, laughing and crying at the
same time.

"The queen's spell only works during the day," the oldest brother explained. "As soon as the sun sets, we lose our swan shapes. That's why we must land – if we turned back into princes while we were flying, we would fall down and be killed. We live far away across the sea, and we can only visit the country where we were born for a week in the summer, when the days are longest. This was our last day.

Tomorrow, we must fly away again."

"Take me with you!" cried Elisa. "Perhaps I can find a way to break the spell."

All night, Elisa and her brothers wove a net from the branches of willow trees that grew on the banks of the stream. The net was finished just before the sun rose. Elisa was so tired that when she lay down in the net, she fell asleep at once.

The rays of the rising sun touched the princes and turned them into swans. The swans picked up the net in their beaks and flew into the sky.

Elisa woke in the late afternoon. The sun was creeping down towards the horizon and there was no land in sight. Storm clouds were gathering, flashing lightning down into the waves. Elisa looked all around, knowing that if the sun set when her brothers were flying, they would turn into men and they would all fall into the sea and drown.

Half the sun was gone when Elisa saw a black rock sticking up out of the waves, looking no bigger than the head of a seal. The swans dived down to the rock and landed. The last of the sun slid out of sight, and when the swans became Elisa's brothers, there was just enough rock for them all on the tiny island. They stood around Elisa, arm in arm, while the storm roared in their ears.

At dawn, the swans flew away from the rock with the net held in their beaks. All day they flew, until they reached the shores of the country where they lived. As the sun was setting, the swans landed in front of a cave.

"This is the Cave of Dreams," said Elisa's youngest brother. "What you dream when you sleep here will show you how to make your wishes come true."

"My only wish is to break the queen's wicked spell," Elisa told him. She fell asleep in the cave and dreamed that she was back in the forest with the old woman who had been gathering berries; only in the dream, the old woman's basket was filled with stinging nettles.

"Your brothers can be freed if you are strong and brave enough," said the old woman. "You see these nettles? Only these or the nettles that grow in churchyards will do. When you pick them, they will sting you, but you must not give up."

"I won't!" said Elisa.

"Then you must tread on the nettles with your bare feet until they are soft enough to make twine," the old woman went on. "Make eleven shirts from the nettle-twine, throw them over the heads of the swans and the spell will break. But remember this – from the moment you begin your task until it is finished, you must not speak. If you say so much as one word, it will stab through your brothers' hearts like a knife and they will die."

Elisa woke up. She left the cave and found the place where nettles grew. Their stings burned her fingers as she picked them, but she shut her lips tight and made no complaint. She trod the nettles with her bare feet, and when they were soft she wound them into a ball of twine.

Elisa's brothers visited her at sunset. At first, they were worried by her silence, but when they saw the strange work she was doing and the hot red blisters on her fingers, they guessed that it was for them, and they left her alone.

Elisa worked all night. She had just finished one shirt when she heard hunting horns and the barkings of dogs nearby. Elisa rolled the shirt and nettles into a bundle and hid in the mouth of the cave. To her horror, a dog came leaping through the bushes.

Other dogs followed it, and then
a band of hunters appeared. The
handsomest of the hunters was the king
of the country. When he caught sight of
Elisa, he got down from his horse and
walked towards her, smiling.

"Who are you?" he asked.

Elisa shook her head and said nothing.

"This cave is no place for beauty like yours," said the king. "Come to my palace. I'll have you dressed in the finest clothes and give you delicious food to eat."

Elisa could not say no. The king lifted her up on to his horse and led her to his palace.

Elisa let serving-women bathe her. They dressed her in silk, wound strings of pearls in her hair and covered her blistered hands with a pair of satin gloves. She looked so beautiful that when she appeared in the royal banqueting hall, all the noblemen bowed low – except the archbishop.

"Don't be taken in by her!" he told the king. "It's my opinion that she's a witch, and she's used her beauty to cast a spell over you."

But the king paid no attention to the archbishop. He took Elisa by the hand and announced that she would be his wife. He led her through the palace and showed her every room.

Elisa stayed silent. Her face was sad – all she could think of was her brothers and her unfinished task.

The last room the king showed her was tiny. In the room lay the shirt, the ball of twine and the bundle of nettles from the cave.

"I could tell they were important to you, so I had them brought here because I thought it might make you happy," said the king.

Elisa smiled at him, and kissed his hand to show how grateful she was. She loved the handsome king, who was so kind to her, but she didn't dare to tell him how she felt.

They were married by the archbishop, who scowled throughout the wedding. When Elisa was made queen, the archbishop pressed the crown so hard on to her head that it hurt, but she made no complaint.

During the day, Elisa stayed by the king's side. At night, she crept into her tiny room to weave the nettles into shirts. Before she had finished the seventh, there were no nettles left.

Quietly, Elisa left the palace. She walked in the moonlight until she came to a graveyard where many nettles grew, waving their heads in the night wind. Though their stings burned like flames, Elisa gathered as many as she could carry.

One person saw her – the archbishop.
He couldn't sleep that night and he
looked through his bedroom window
just as Elisa was returning. The next
morning, he told the king what he
had seen.

"Your new wife is a witch, just as I
told you!" said the archbishop. "If she
leaves the palace again, we'll follow her."

Days went by. Elisa had finished ten shirts, but she didn't have a single nettle left. Once more, she left the palace and walked to the graveyard.

This time, the king and the archbishop were behind her. They watched her picking the nettles that grew among the headstones.

"She's a witch!" hissed the archbishop. "She must be burned at the stake!"

The king rushed forward and took Elisa in his arms.

"Tell me it's not true, I beg you!" he begged her.

But Elisa said nothing, though she longed to explain.

With tears in his eyes, the king returned to the palace and gave orders for Elisa to be taken to prison. Her fine silk clothes were taken away and she was dressed in sacking. She was given the shirts she had woven and her bundle of nettles to sleep on, instead of a pillow and sheets.

Elisa made no protest. Tears streamed down her face as she carried on weaving the last shirt. She was still weaving it at dawn, when soldiers came to march her into the courtyard. In the centre of the yard, firewood had been heaped up into a high pile. Near the firewood, the archbishop stood with the king and all the nobles.

"Burn the witch!" shrieked the archbishop. "And make sure all her foul magic burns with her!"

The soldiers threw the ten nettle-twine shirts at Elisa's feet, but they let her hold on to the eleventh, which she kept on weaving. The executioner reached out for her.

Suddenly there was a great clattering
of wings. Eleven wild swans, with gold
crowns on their heads, flew down out
of the sky and pecked the executioner
until he staggered backwards. Quickly,
Elisa dropped the shirts over the swans,
and there stood her brothers. The
youngest still had a swan's wing,
because Elisa had not quite finished
the last shirt.

"Our sister is no witch!" the youngest brother told the king. "She was working to free us from an evil spell!"

"At last, I can speak!" sighed Elisa. "It's true! I'm innocent!"

At the sound of her voice, the sticks of firewood cracked open and red roses grew out of them. At the top of the heap was a white flower, gleaming like a star. The king picked the flower and gave it to Elisa.

"Ring every church bell in the land!" he said to the archbishop. "Let all the people celebrate in honour of my brave queen and her brothers."

And that night in the palace, the king held the biggest feast that had ever been seen.